2010
Happy Halloween!

Love,

Grandma
&
Grandpa

DAVID GETZ

FLOATING HOME

ILLUSTRATED BY MICHAEL REX

HENRY HOLT AND COMPANY • NEW YORK

This book is for the astronauts Colonel Steve Nagel,
Marsha Ivans, and Dr. Leroy Chiao

And for Jacqui and Maxine,
who will need no rocket ship to see
the world as something strange and new.

—D. G.

To my father, for the movies
—M. R.

Henry Holt and Company, LLC
Publishers since 1866
175 Fifth Avenue
New York, New York 10010
www.HenryHoltKids.com

Library of Congress Cataloging-in-Publication Data
Getz, David. Floating home / David Getz; illustrated by Michael Rex.
Summary: To look at her home in a new way for an art project,
eight-year-old Maxine rides on a space shuttle, where she experiences the
many thrills of takeoff and has the opportunity to indeed view her home,
Earth, in an entirely new way.
[1. Space shuttles—Fiction. 2. Home—Fiction.] I. Rex, Michael, ill. II. Title.
PZ7.G3299Fl 1996 [Fic]—dc20 96-14220

ISBN-13: 978-0-8050-6580-0 / ISBN-10: 0-8050-6580-6
10 9 8 7 6 5 4 3

First published in hardcover in 1997 by Henry Holt and Company
First paperback edition—2000
The artist used acrylic on cel vinyl to create the illustrations for this book.
Printed in China on acid-free paper. ∞

When Mrs. Selinsky asked the class to look at their homes in a new way and to draw what they saw, Maxine left school and kept on walking.

She passed Kevin outside his house, sitting on the branch of a tree, studying his home as if he were a squirrel.

She passed Selina lying in the grass in her front yard, looking up at her apartment building as if she were an ant.

She passed Oscar in dark sunglasses, standing in front of his home, pretending he was a stranger.

Artist's pad under her arm, her unsharpened colored pencils in their box, and a globe sharpener with all the countries of the world in her overalls pocket, Maxine passed her own home and kept on walking.

She was going to draw the most unusual picture of all, a picture of the earth from space. She was going to be the youngest astronaut of all time!

KENNEDY SPACE CENTER
at Cape Canaveral in Florida

Maxine checked into her room, wrote a letter to her mom and dad, and undressed to take a shower.

She knew it would be the last shower she would take for two weeks.

You don't shower in the space shuttle. Water does not fall from the nozzle.

Nothing falls inside a shuttle in space. Water spraying out of a shower would float all over the place and quickly fill the cabin with dancing beads of liquid.

Maxine turned on the hot water. She let herself disappear in a cloud of steam.

She washed her hair.

She opened a window to let the steam escape.

Her last breakfast on Earth was in three hours.

Her crewmates ate very little.

Maxine had a cup of orange juice and a bowl of cereal.

She was disappointed there was no prize in her cereal box. She watched the milk pour from the container. Down it flowed. Down.

Soon there would be no down in the shuttle. Down is where things fall.

In space, nothing falls.

She couldn't pour milk in space.

Suddenly newspaper and television reporters burst into the room.

"Maxine!" one of them called out. "Are you afraid?"

"Maxine," another asked, "how does it feel to be the first eight-year-old astronaut?"

"Maxine, are you going to miss your parents?"

"Maxine, why are you doing it?"

"Art," Maxine told them. "I'm doing it for art."

"Time to get dressed!" said a NASA official.

It was the biggest diaper she had ever seen.

"You gotta wear it," a woman from NASA told her. "You could be sitting in your seat waiting to launch for hours. You can't raise your hand and ask to go. Then, a few minutes after you launch and the shuttle's zipping ahead, you're going to be pushed back into your seat and you're not going to be able to move, and it's going to feel like something very heavy is sitting on your bladder. Then . . ."

"Got the point," Maxine said.

She put on long thermal underwear in case she got too cold. On top of her thermal underwear she put on her cooling underwear, in case she began to overheat. The cooling suit had little tubes of water sewn in the bottom and the top. It looked like a Spider-Man costume.

"Don't tell my classmates about the diaper," she said.

"No problem," the woman said.

She braided her hair so that it would fit into the helmet.

More reporters were waiting for her in the suit room. They were there to watch her get dressed.

She was glad this didn't happen at home every morning.

The pressure suit was meant to protect her should anything happen to the shuttle before it rose to nineteen miles above the ground. The suit was big and orange, and she didn't put it on as much as climb into it. Through a slit in the back Maxine shoved one leg, then the other, and then her arms. She poked her head through the tight neck band at the top of the suit. The boots locked onto the pants cuffs. The gloves locked onto the sleeves, and the helmet locked onto the collar.

The people from NASA put all sorts of things in her pockets: special gloves to keep her warm if she needed to parachute out of the shuttle and land in the ocean; an emergency radio; survival gear; sharpener and colored pencils. They also gave her a small mirror.

"Place it on your lap," someone said. "You'll be able to see out the window above your head."

It was time to go out to the pad.

 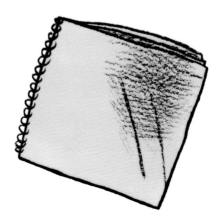

Feeling like a hundred-pound duck in a diaper, Maxine waddled over to the van that would take her to the launch pad.

It was 3 A.M. and dark outside. Maxine had never been outside at 3 A.M. before.

"So this is what the world looks like when I'm sleeping," she said to herself.

And then she saw the shuttle. It was alive.

Suspended above the pad, the vehicle was lit by dazzlingly bright xenon lights as if it were an actor, stage center, ready for his big speech.

And it was breathing. Exhaling steam from its top and bottom, it reminded Maxine of a dragon.

The orbiter itself looked like a stubby airplane. It rode piggyback on a huge orange fuel tank as tall as a fifteen-story building. Filled with liquid hydrogen and oxygen, the orange tank would supply the fuel for the shuttle's main engines.

On either side of the orange tank were the two solid rocket boosters. Loaded with chunks of solid fuel like skyscrapers stuffed with gunpowder, these boosters would help lift the shuttle off the pad and into space.

Maxine entered the shuttle's orbiter through a porthole. Since the shuttle was pointed straight up, ready for launch, the back wall was actually her floor. To protect the panels and instruments from the astronauts' heavy feet, the wall was covered with a thick pad.

"Some art project," a technician said, and helped strap Maxine into her seat.

"I hope your mom puts your drawing on her refrigerator," another technician said, and checked her suit. He made sure it was in working order.

The technicians removed the padding covering the back wall and, one by one, stepped out through the porthole.

As the door closed, Maxine checked to make sure her pad, pencils, and sharpener were still there.

The countdown began.

With two minutes to go, the controllers at Cape Canaveral announced over the radio, "Close and lock your visors. Turn on your suit oxygen. Have a nice flight."

Maxine placed the mirror on her lap. She could see through the window above her head. She saw nothing but clouds and a clear blue sky.

Then she did as she was told. She lowered her visor and began to breathe oxygen from her suit.

The main engines started. Everything began to tremble. It was a familiar feeling, like being in a subway train. The vibrations jostled her mirror.

Then the whole shuttle began to sway.

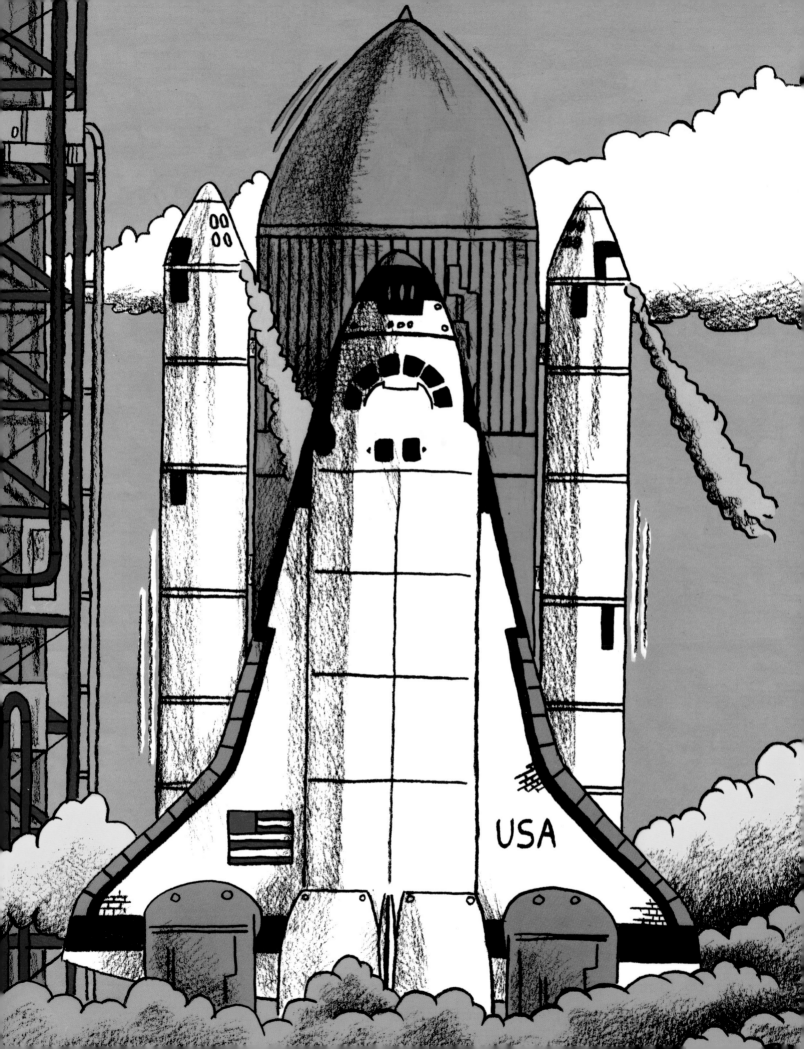

Suddenly the rumbling became thunderous; the gentle subway became an earthquake. Everything shuddered and shook.

The shuttle swayed back. The solid rockets ignited.

The noise!

Like a thousand thousand lions roaring! Like the heart of an immense raging fire. *Roar!*

Boom!

She was pressed deep into her seat.

Then something kicked her in the back.

Then . . . up!

"We are going!" she told herself. "We are definitely going somewhere!"

Up! Up!
Launch!
Looking into her mirror, she could see the launch pad dropping away at a dizzying speed. Rapidly everything on the ground became smaller and smaller.
Up! Up!

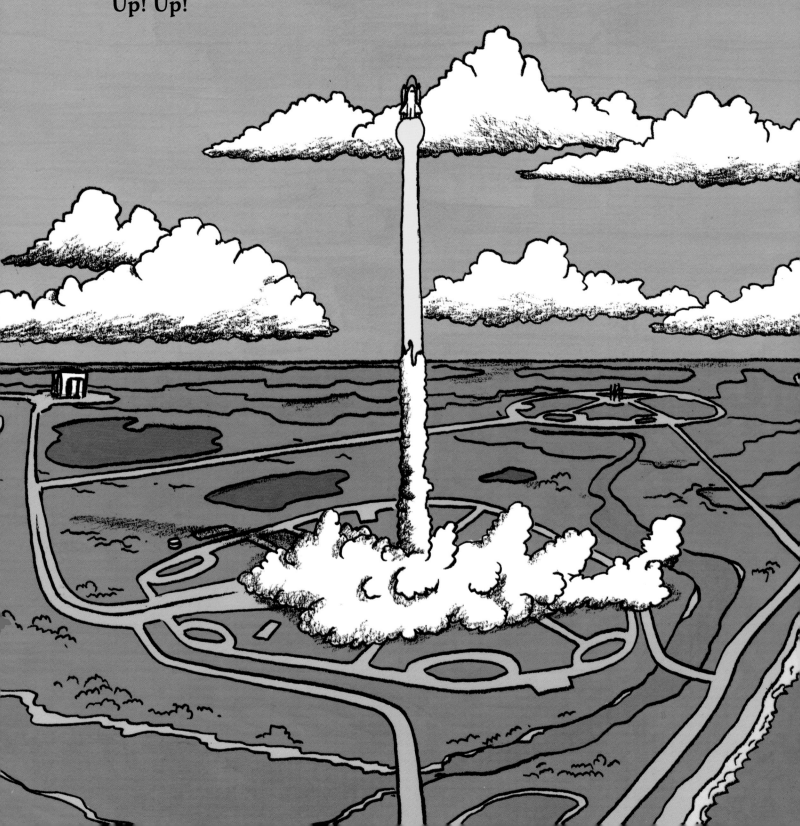

One . . . two . . . three . . . four . . . five . . . six . . . seven . . .
flying faster and faster . . . eight! The shuttle began to roll.
Over, then over.
Maxine watched the sunlight fly across the cabin.
She was flying upside down.
Invisible hands pushed her deep into her seat.
The shuttle hurtled through the thick atmosphere.
The wind howled.

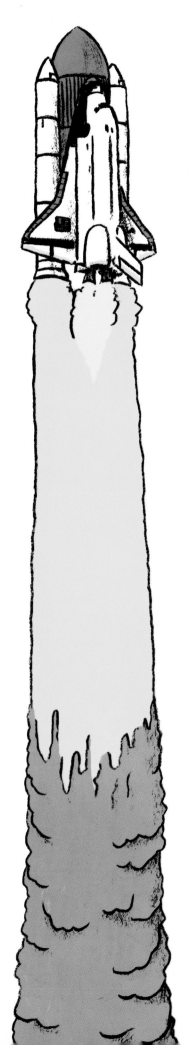

In twenty seconds she was traveling faster than the speed of sound, faster than the word *hello* travels from one person's mouth to another's ear— 760 miles per hour! One mile every five seconds!

Faster, then faster. The shuttle tore through the thick atmosphere.

At two minutes, their fuel completely used up, the solid rocket boosters were no longer necessary. It was time to get rid of them.

Bang! The separation motors jettisoned the solid rocket boosters away from the shuttle. It felt like a giant had whacked the shuttle with a big stick.

The cabin lit up. For a frightening second everything was fire and smoke outside the windows.

Then clear.

Then quiet.

Maxine imagined the empty rocket canisters under their parachutes, drifting back down to Earth. They would be picked up in the ocean.

Now the ride was glass smooth. And impossibly fast.
  Within eight minutes of launch, Maxine was traveling 11,000 miles per hour, or almost 190 miles a minute. Three miles a second.
  The acceleration continued to press her deep into her seat, made her face feel as if a heavy weight were pushing against it, made her chest feel as if a gorilla were sitting on her ribs.
  It was hard to breathe. She took quick, shallow, sharp breaths.
  She couldn't move, couldn't lift her arms.
  Then the three main engines cut off.

Suddenly everything was funny. In less than a heartbeat, Maxine went from feeling as if she weighed two hundred pounds to feeling as if she weighed nothing at all.

She was in space.

Her eyes seemed to float in her head. Her stomach floated in her belly. She floated within her suit.

She felt giddy . . . and a little sick.

"We made it!"

Someone laughed.

All around the cabin, things were floating. Checklists attached to panels by strings drifted like sea plants. Her mirror gently tumbled over and over through the air of the cabin.

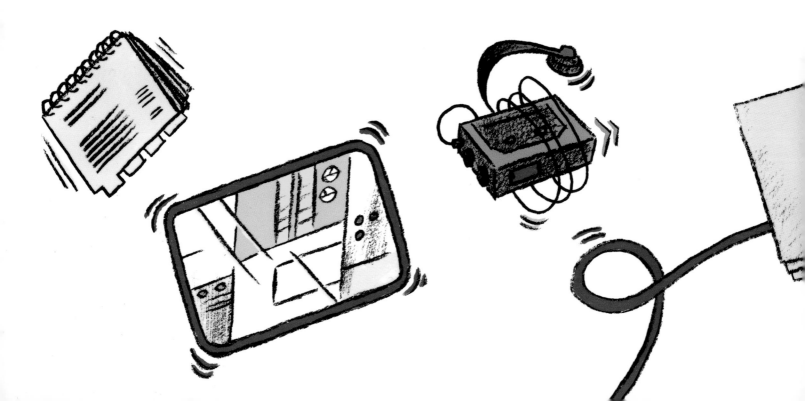

"Maxine," someone called to her, "look up!" There in the window was Earth.

It was dazzling, sitting like a royal-blue gem on black velvet.

At its curved edge, on the horizon, was a thin, bright, fluorescent-blue band. The atmosphere.

She was looking down at the air she had breathed.

Somewhere down there her house sat at the bottom of the atmosphere. Her parents were breathing its air.

Suddenly something drew a long, thin streak beneath her.

It was a shooting star. A chunk of rock from space had sliced through the atmosphere and burned up.

She was looking down at the shooting stars.

The shuttle passed over a funnel of clouds, a hurricane. Where the sky was clear, she could see shades of brown, gray, green. All that blue.

But where was her home? Where was her town, her city? Her state? She removed her globe sharpener, with all the countries.

She looked out the window. Somebody had forgotten to draw in the lines! Where were the lines that divided up the continents into countries? Where were the lines that divided up the countries into states, the states into cities?

There were no lines. It was just one Earth.

It was her home.